SUSPENSE STORIES V4

GREAT SUSPENSE STORIES

ABDUL RAHIM KHURRAM

Contents

CHAPTER ONE

I'm gonna fly

“Hey, John,” a voice calls from behind and I curse under my breath. I was hoping to get to my car before he’d followed me downstairs.

“Sorry, Winston, I have somewhere to be,” I pant, stealing a glance at him. His face is red, not from the heat, but from our boss yelling at him for the last 10 minutes.

“Where have you got to be? You never go anywhere,” Winston protests, and then his voice lowers, “you kind of threw me under the bus back there, man.”

“Sorry, Winston, I don’t have time to talk right now. I’ll see you tomorrow,” I say, jogging to my vehicle.

I sigh as I shut myself into my Jetta, avoiding eye contact as I drive past my friend. It’s not like I lied, I just let our boss think that he miscalculated the numbers, not me. What was I supposed to do? I’ve never been one for confrontation, he knows that.

I’m waiting to turn left into my apartment when I see it, a dark ominous cloud hanging over the outskirts of town. I squint into it, I’ve never seen clouds so dark before, the blackness is so full it feels supernatural.

An aggressive honking snaps me out of the trance and I hit the gas hard, causing my car to shudder and squeal its way into the complex. I groan when I find my parking spot once again inhabited. I peel around and reverse into my roommate's spot on the far end of the lot.

"Fucking Mathews," I grumble as I pull my briefcase out of the trunk. I think of a new curse for Mathews for every extra step it takes to my front door. Letting myself in with a huff, I find the culprit lounging on the couch with a beer in one hand and a cigarette in the other.

"Mathews, you parked in my spot again."

"Oh, yeah sorry about that, Pete," Mathews takes a swig of his beverage, "see, I had to bring in the groceries. You don't expect me to walk all the way from the end of the lot with all the groceries, do you? You've only got that there briefcase."

"Well, I guess," I reply, shuffling my feet.

"Yeah, glad we got it figured out," Mathews grins and lumbers over to the fridge, "want a drink?"

"Uh, sure," I wave my hand, my attention is drawn to the television. The news is covering the storm clouds I saw on my way home, claiming that they will be on us this evening. "Did you see we're about to have a storm?"

"Yeah, the weatherman says to expect torrential weather for a good week at least. They look pretty menacing hey?"

I nod with a gulp. I've never experienced a storm like this and have no idea what to expect.

A few hours later Mathews announces that he's going to the bar with some friends, leaving me alone in the apartment. Despite the thunder rumbling outside, I manage to distract myself with a movie. At some point between the end of the film and the bottom of the popcorn bowl, I drift off.

I sit up on the couch, shivering. The television is still playing, but the sound is muffled as if my head were underwater. Something is wrong with the screen; the picture keeps flickering between the baseball film and NBP's news coverage of the storm. Something seems to be taking shape within the storm. Goosebumps begin to prickle on the back of my neck as the form of a woman emerges, her eyes slits of red. She raises a hand, pointing at me, and appears to be talking but no voice can be heard. I snatch up the remote control, rapidly punching the power button but the woman does not disappear. Instead, a crimson smile spreads across her features.

"Are you ready to fly?" A deep, multitoned voice whispers in my ear, and I jolt awake.

I look at the television and the credits to the Million Dollar Arm are playing across the screen. Once I've finally stopped shaking, I stand up. Maybe moving into my bedroom would be more conducive to sleep. A scream erupts from somewhere overhead, distantly at first but growing stronger and stronger until there's a terrible thud and then silence. I cover my ears and run to my room, slamming the door shut behind me.

In the comfort of my bed, I attempt to process what's just happened. Most likely, the scream was some late-night partiers getting up to no good. And the dream, well, that's just a culmination of my anxiety and the storm. With these soothing explanations, I finally manage to fall into a deep slumber.

As I leave for work the next morning, I'm surprised to see that, despite the clouds hanging heavy overhead, it is not raining. But even more startling is the yellow tape wrapped around the side of the building accompanied by a slew of officers and hazmat suits. I take a few steps forward to see the scene from a better angle and instantly wish I hadn't. Right outside my kitchen window is an occupied body bag.

"Excuse me, sir," I look up and find myself face to face with a police officer, "sir, this is a crime scene. Unless you have some information for us, I'm going to have to ask you to move along."

All I can manage is a nod. My eyes fixate on a woman adorned in a hazmat suit crouches over the body. Her head slowly raises, allowing me to see her face. She seems to notice me because her mouth curls into a smile and her tongue darts out across her lips, causing ruby droplets to parade down her chin.

"Sir, are you alright?" The officer asks.

"Huh?"

"You look unwell, are you okay?"

I look between the officer and the body—the woman has disappeared. I shake my head and stumble to my vehicle. The entire drive to work I spend reasoning with myself and once I've arrived, I'm feeling confident that I must have just imagined her as a result of the nightmare I'd had the evening before.

I hasten inside to my cubicle but find that I needn't have hurried at all. The workroom is in complete chaos. Just as I'm about to sit, Winston rushes over, "John, oh man am I glad to see you. I heard that one of the suicides was in your building."

"Wait, what? One of the suicides?"

"You haven't heard?" Winston gasps, "there was a mass suicide last night. Eight men jumped off buildings across town."

"No way! Eight?" I open the news on my desktop. Sure enough, news station is covering it. NBP has collaged 8 different crime scenes, each with its own body bag set at the bottom of a building. I spot my apartment and bring my face close to the screen. She's not in the picture. The station changes back to the weather and Cindy Wimbledon is front and center. The image flickers and Cindy is replaced by a woman, shrouded in black. She snarls and runs her tongue across her teeth.

I grab Winston's shoulder and point at the computer, "do you see her? Look, it's her!"

"Who, the weather woman? Yeah, I see her."

"No, not the fucking weather woman," I shriek. The impersonator winks at me and then it flickers again and NBP's blonde, blue-eyed weather woman is staring back at us. "What the fuck. What kind of game is this?" I yank my glasses off my nose and swipe at my forehead.

"John, you don't look so good. Maybe you should go home?" Winston says, backing out of my cubicle.

"Fuck off, Winston. I'm not crazy!" I spit.

Winston raises his hands in submission, "go home, John. I'll tell them you're sick."

Maybe he's right. If I'm sick it would explain why I'm seeing all this crazy shit.

My sick day was spent reading a book. If I don't turn on the television she can't come through the screen. Not that she's real. She's not. But I'd rather not give my imagination the chance to play tricks on me. At 5PM Mathews lumbers into the apartment, "I see you took my parking spot," he chuckles, taking a beer from the fridge.

"It's not your spot."

"I know, pal. I'm just pulling your leg."

"I'd prefer you didn't."

Mathews does a flippant motion with his hands and plops himself down on the couch. He flicks on the television and instantly NBP News is on the screen, "it's raining again," he muses, observing the weather forecast.

"I-it is?"

Mathews nods and takes a swig of his beer, "They're talking about those suicides. The guy that jumped off our building was the one from the corner unit, Hank I think his name was."

I gulp and turn to see the shortlist of names, "Hank, that's right."

"All men hey? It makes one a little nervous," Mathews shifts and frowns.

"What do you mean? They were suicides, weren't they?"

"I guess."

The woman's face flashes across my mind, the glee as she knelt over Hank's body was palpable. I shudder and stand, "I'm going to bed."

"To bed? It's not even 5:30," Mathews says, sitting up, "I was hoping you'd hang here tonight."

"Sorry, Mathews. I came home sick today. I'm going to bed." I shut myself into my room and crawl into bed. If I go to sleep maybe I can avoid hearing the storm outside and avoid any nightmares.

I'm outside of my complex looking at the crime scene again but this time, it's pouring rain. There are police officers scattered all around, but I can't make out any of their faces, they're shrouded in darkness, as if their hoods are filled with fog. I turn to look at Hank's body bag, it's exactly where I remember. I stumble towards it, my feet sloshing through puddles. I kneel in front of the bag and take hold of the zipper, pulling it down. A tuft of brown hair emerges, and I pause, Hank is a redhead. All I want is to run, to get as far from this gory scene as possible, yet I can't. My hand continues to reveal the face. My heart stops in horror as a pair of glasses come into view, framing blank, hazel eyes. I know who it is, but still, my hand moves on, as if I can't confirm the identity without seeing the whole of his face. The zipper slides over a familiar nose, an unmistakable pair of lips until the entire head is revealed.

"Are you ready to jump?" The deep voice growls and I know who it is before even looking.

"No, no, not me. Anyone but me!" I wail.

"Who then?"

My eyes fly open, and the woman is there, hovering in the corner of my room. She has an amused expression on her face as if she's playing with a new toy. The room is unnaturally dark, there is no light save for the ominous red glow that she emits.

"No, no, this can't be real."

"Someone will die tonight. If not you, then who?"

The words leave my mouth before I've had time to even consider them, "m-my roommate, Mathews. Just spare me, please," I whimper, clasping my hands in earnest.

She bites her bottom lip, swaying from side to side like a puppet on a string. A smile spreads across her face and with a flash, she's gone.

The room warms and brightens but despite the now comfortable temperature, I can't stop shivering. I must have been hallucinating, ghosts aren't real. She can't be real. And yet, I hear Mathews's door creak and the soft padding of his feet. The front door opens and closes and then I hear nothing. He's just going out for drinks with his friends. She isn't real. She isn't real. She isn't....

There's a scream, small at first, then growing louder and louder until, with a sickening thud, everything goes quiet.

Sleep denied me last night. I keep hoping that when I leave my room I'll find Mathews, frying eggs or brushing his teeth, but when I've finally worked up the courage to step foot into the living room, I'm met with an eerie silence. "Mathews?" I call, but there is no answer.

I swing open the front door, sprinting out, my bathrobe billowing out behind me. The pavement is sharp on my bare feet as I run around the corner, and then I see it. Mathews's body was crushed and broken, a pool of drying blood embracing him. There is a slew of people in uniforms taping off the area. An officer seems to notice me and begins to approach but I rush back into the apartment and then crumple to the floor.

I stay curled up on the tile for what seems like hours when there's a knock at the door, "John? It's me, Winston." I bring myself to my feet and open the door to see my workmate, "oh thank god, Pete! I heard someone in your building jumped last night, there were 11 last night, did you hear? When you didn't show up to work, I was worried."

"11 people?" I whisper, slumping into the kitchen chair in shock. Winston nods sorrowfully and I pull on my hair, "Mathews was one of them."

"What? Like, Mathews your roommate?" He gasps and I nod, "did you hear anything?Have you made a report?"

"What? No."

"You haven't done anything at all?"

"You know what, Winston? I don't need your fucking judgment. My roommate just died. It wasn't my fault. Just get out," I yell, shoving the man out the door then slamming it in his face. I throw myself onto the sofa, once again, sink into a restless sleep.

I'm awoken by the clapping of thunder and an intense chill coming over the room. I sit up, groping for a blanket when there's a low chuckle, "you won't be needing that."

I open my eyes and find my breath is stolen from my lungs. She's floating above my face, her hands propped up under her chin, "Are you ready to jump?"

"What? I-I gave you Mathews. What more do you want from me?"

"I need a sacrifice," she hisses, her eyes flaming.

She rushes down and wraps her hands around my throat. "Winston!" I sputter, "take Winston." Her lips curl into a smile and then she disappears.

I haven't been to work since the day before Mathews's death, so I haven't had to witness Winston's empty cubicle. Maybe I would've been able to stomach it if I'd had the chance to forget the storm witch, but she has visited me every night for a week. Giving her names was difficult at first, but as time went on it became easier. I began to list people who had bullied me in school, or my mother's ex-boyfriends, and I've begun to find it rather gratifying. Lounging on the couch, I flick on the television. NBP is once again covering the alleged suicides and there is Cindy in all her golden glory.

"The term 'It's Been Raining Men,' has never been so true, as our city has been struck with a catastrophic rise in male suicides," she recites, and I can't help but chuckle. She proceeds to list the names of the men who had died the previous evening. I feel a jolt of satisfaction when I see the name I'd chosen, Gerald Vickerson, my old highschool teacher who had failed me in Math class.

"Despite these dark times, I have some good news," Cindy forces a smile, "we will be seeing the sun again here in Phoenix. The winds have changed, and the storm is making its way south."

I sit up straight, a manic grin spreading across my face. If the storm leaves, she must leave. I'll be free. No one will ever become aware of my part to play in this massacre. Suddenly there is a clap of thunder and the sound of rain battering against my window draws my attention away from the television.

There is a creaking sound from behind me and I sit rigid, unable to look. It's her, I know it. And yet, there is a strange sound, like she is dragging something behind her.

"John," a man's voice croons. It can't be. "You killed us, John."

I open my mouth to scream but nothing comes out. There, crawling in through my front door is Winston and Mathews and seven other men whose names I had bestowed to the woman. Their bodies are broken and bent at unearthly angles. Mathews's head is lolling to the side and half of Winston's face is missing. Blood slides out from beneath the men, staining my tile flooring. "N-no, it, it wasn't my fault," I stammer.

"You betrayed us. And now, it's time for you to fly."

The men break into a chorus, chanting, "time to fly," over and over.

Covering my ears, I turn to flee but a bloodied, deformed hand grabs my pant leg and I come crashing down to the floor. They're almost on me when the black cloud appears over my head, the woman floating within it, her face twisted in delight.

"Are you ready to jump?" She blows a kiss, and black smoke envelops me.

The ground beneath me changes, no longer soft carpet, but rough and gritty. I look around and find myself on the roof of my apartment.

"No," I plead as my body moves on its own to stand on the edge of the roof.

"Time to fly," she commands.

My feet slip off into nothingness and I plummet towards the earth.

Turns out, I can't fly.

CHAPTER TWO

In a Clean and Appropriate Manner

He was sitting by himself, reading. The novel's cover was taken off. The first page was also almost torn off. It seemed to be kept on by a single strand of hair. He got up a bit, but something in his thoughts made him sit down again. He had no idea what the book was about. He couldn't resist discovering additional pages that he was inadvertently skipping. He discovered the book next to a towel. A soiled towel, to be sure. An orange, dirt-splattered, soiled towel. On the inside of the book, there were scribbles and comments, but the title and author were missing. It was as if they had been deleted from the book. The book made no sense; it was as if the book was directing someone to do something but not telling you what you were directed to do.

In this world, he was alone. That was his frame of mind. Johnny was his given name. He wasn't accepted in school, and he didn't have a place to live. He shared a room with a student who did not talk. He's never heard them say anything. Maybe once, but he doesn't recall hearing her voice even if she did. Nonnie was her name. Johnny's mother was aware that she did not have a house. His parents vanished one day. Were were drugs involved? Was it madness? Johnny had no idea. He just knew his parents had stopped loving him and themselves and had moved to a location where they could be alone. Johnny was unaware of the relationship between Nonnie's parents and his own, but the tie seemed to be strong since he was welcomed at the Hartshorn's house. Nonnie Hartshorn and her mother Josh Hartshorn have unusual names. They could have thought Johnny's name was weird, but Johnny wouldn't mind if they did. He was little and invisible, with a feeble appearance. In everything they did, everyone appeared to be one step ahead of Johnny.

It was October, and the moon seemed to be carried away by a puppeteer. It started in one area and then moved to another. Johnny has a fascination with the moon since he was a child in Magnolien. The moon shone brightly in Magnolien. It was a charming name for a depressing place. Johnny like watching a variety of things, particularly slow things. Johnny liked visiting to one specific store. It was a clock store, and Johnny was always captivated by the many sorts of clocks for sale. But he never purchased them. Johnny has always wanted to own a clock store. It wasn't a dream shared by others. Johnny used to look at Johnny's mother's clock. It was simply a regular clock, but Johnny was drawn to the deep blue hue. He was expressionless and stolid as he glanced at the clock. Johnny was a rapid thinker who always knew what to do or say, thus many things seemed sluggish to him. For a long time, Johnny thought that staring at a clock made time slow down. Perhaps that was true.

The earth was shrouded in fog. It was late, and Johnny had gone out to get some chocolate from a candy shop. After that, he planned to visit the clock business and enjoy some chocolate with the owner, Ridley. Johnny and Ridley were close friends. He went to the clock store after purchasing wonderful, dark, but dulcet chocolate. Johnny was always warmed by the rusting metal lettering spelling out "Cerulean's" over the entrance. Johnny enjoyed the rich blue hue of the carpet, despite the fact that he was wearing shoes. He attempted to open the door, but it seemed to be closed. The lights were on on inside, but the door would not open. Johnny was depressed and returned home. He was exhausted from his trek. He generally rested at the store, which was somewhat far away. He had to travel the whole distance without stopping now that it was closed. More chocolate for himself, he reasoned. He nibbled into the chocolate. He constantly purchased the same chocolate bar, yet it never grew old to him.

Johnny was walking to school the next day. Something unusual occurred at this point. He ran into a strange guy, or rather, the man rushed into him. Actually, let's just say both. They ran into each other. Johnny wasn't paying attention to what was in front of him. The guy could have simply avoided Johnny, but he didn't. Johnny didn't seem to notice and continued going. When he was bumped into by a lady this time, Johnny decided to widen his eyes wide and go straight and around anybody. He apologised for running into her. The unusual bump frightened the lady, but when Johnny apologised, she didn't appear to notice. Johnny kept going and understood he had to avoid everyone. Everyone continued going without recognising him. Johnny was perplexed. He rang the bell to gain access to the school, and he saw instructors inside who were perplexed. He had the impression that he was being neglected by everyone. What could he have done so spectacularly that the whole town ignored him? Did the whole community turn a blind eye to him because of his appearance? Johnnys' dark golden brown hair seemed to be normal. His long, tangled hair seemed to be the same as it did every day. He was unconcerned about the opinions of others. His clothing were tidy yet tattered. His dark, blood-red sneakers seemed natural. The laces had been torn into many threads, as though they had all been knotted together to form the lace. Everything around him seemed to be normal. What was going on? His wide round green eyes tightened with concern. He skipped school and dashed straight home to check on the Hartshorns.

Johnny had returned to their home, and neither Nonnie nor Josh had spotted him. Nonnie never went to school. She's... unusual. Johnny hasn't seen her at school in years, and the only time he's seen her is when she comes out of her room and goes back in. This time she was out of her room and didn't even glance at him. It was true at the time that no one saw or heard Johnny. Johnny knew they wouldn't overlook him like that. Johnny was at a loss about what to do. On the one hand, this may have been beneficial to Johnny. He'd always longed to be able to disappear. He realised he wasn't even invisible anymore, that he had vanished from people's thoughts, that he had been forgotten. He realised after some thought that he couldn't live like way forever. He needed everything to return to normal. He reasoned that if he approached someone he knew, they would recognise him. He discovered Nonnie in her chamber. Her hair was braided.

"What's going on?" he asks. "Can you hear what I'm saying?"

She glanced at him, opened her lips, paused, and loudly muttered, "What do you need?"

"Can you see me?" Do you hear me? Why is the town so uninterested in me? Why didn't you say anything when

I entered the home again? "I have a lot of questions!" he exclaimed, loudly.

She didn't seem perplexed, but she was. Nonnie was often expressionless. Almost like Johnny seeing his mother's cerulean clock.

"Well, I don't know, because I haven't been invisible lately," she said humorously.

Johnny was terrified, yet relieved that he had met someone with whom he could communicate. He'd never been happier to live with Nonnie. They spoke for a while, and Nonnie disclosed that she had been reading a lot of witch-related novels. Johnny shuddered at the idea that this had anything to do with the otherworldly, but he knew it was probably true. Johnny has never been a lover of curses or magic. She said that a curse had been cast by Lierau Taboc, a well-known witch who resided in the darker sections of Medeni, a nearby city. She curses individuals with the curse of disappearance, where no one can see or hear them.

"Impossible, curses don't exist, but even if they did, which they don't, how come you can see and hear me?" Johnny enquired.

"Let's read more," Nonnie shrugged. She said softly.

There was a book published by the witch herself that was an excellent instruction on how to break the spell. Johnny reasoned that it was best to attempt to break the curse even if he didn't know whether he was cursed or not. Johnny had to locate this book. He recalled the book. The book that doesn't have a cover. The witch's novel was the book without an author! He went downstairs to his room, but there was no book. There was dust where he recalled it being. This was dreadful; the book had vanished. He will be cursed for the rest of his life. Did the witch discover he was seeking for the book and steal it? He looked and looked and looked and looked and looked and looked and looked and looked and looked and looked and looked and looked and looked and He saw a little track that led to a small hole in his wall. He touched it with his palm and felt about. A hand gripped him, feeling like tree bark, and pulled until his hand couldn't go any farther. He couldn't take a breath. It felt as though his lips was on his palm and was being covered by whatever this was. Nonnie merely looked, terrified. Johnny collapsed unexpectedly. He was so weak that he couldn't resist the hand pulling him down this hole, which may have been a mouse hole that had mysteriously sprouted in his chamber.

Johnny awoke and examined his surroundings. He couldn't move his limbs and couldn't elevate his head. He turned over to see Nonnie laying there, staring at him. He wasn't in any discomfort, and he wasn't bleeding. His limbs and legs had shrunk to the size of little pimples. Johnny had never been in such a state of disbelief before, yet he wasn't terrified. He rolled closer to Nonnie until he touched her, at which point everything he saw became white. He blinked, and he was back in his room, this time screaming in agony as the bark hand pulled much harder than before. He and the hand both ceased resisting. He eventually came to a halt, and the hand stopped tugging. He became aware of the trend. He pulled it abruptly when he got the opportunity, and his arm was torn off by the hand. Nonnie screamed and ran to Johnny. Johnny closed his eyes once again, realising that what he had seen previously might have been his future. When he opened his eyes, he was back to the hand that was tugging him. Was this a riddle? Why did he keep returning to this point in time? He and the hand both ceased resisting. He was at a loss for what to do. He believed that the best solution was to just wait it out, but this may take days. He was aware that if he attempted to take his hand away, it would draw back.

"This had to be a test," Johnny thought anxiously to himself.

He sat in this posture for hours, without moving, until the hand abruptly released go. He spotted the book as he peeked into the hole. Was the witch putting him to the test? He attempted to figure out how to grab the book, but when he felt powerless, a hand came out of the hole and gave him the book's cover.

Johnny read aloud, "Obsolete," in hushed tones.

He glanced down at the hand that had gripped him before, which was now opening up like a flower. When he glanced inside, he saw that another hand was clutching an orange towel with something within it. He grabbed the towel, unwrapped it, and returned the book. The book was utterly bare, and all of the text had vanished. Johnny stepped back. Nonnie remained standing in the same spot.

“Nonnie?” Johnny murmured hesitantly.

She didn't respond. Johnny seems to be broken. He touched her without her noticing. Johnny was now also concealed in her consciousness. He strolled about the house hopelessly, dejected. He didn't care that he was probably making progress any longer. What's the sense of life if you're always alone? He thought he was alone in the world, but he found he wasn't. He just knew now that he was completely alone.

“Johnny?” Josh interrupted his sobs.

"What are you doing with that piece of paper?" she said softly.

Johnny couldn't believe what he was hearing. Josh, did you hear and see him? When he glanced around, everything in the room seemed to be normal. Anyone anyone see or hear Johnny? He rushed outside without saying anything to Josh. He approached someone, and they turned around, stunned. They welcomed him pleasantly. He had no clue what he had done to put a halt to this. He returned home and discovered one of Nonnie's novels. It seemed weighty, although it was quite light. He took out the book and began reading it. It was the account of the same curse he was cursed with. It was broken by passing it on to someone else, someone who accepts the curse; he then recognised it was the same book he had when he discovered it next to the orange towel. The cover had been fitted. Nonnie must have accepted the orange towel and the curse, for the book is now hers.

"Nonnie?" Johnny murmured something.

She seemed to be gone, but was she? Johnny had been cursed, and he understood how it operated. Johnny had a feeling she was someplace. He didn't notice or hear him. He wanted the curse to be removed from him; knowing that Nonnie had intentionally cursed herself for him made him regret being such a coward. The book said that if you really wanted to assist someone with the curse who was in need, you would be cursed. The hand will materialise and provide you with the book. Johnny's life was not cursed for the rest of it. Years passed, and Johnny was constantly sorry of himself for not surrendering his happiness, which he no longer had when Nonnie died. He wanted the hand to return and condemn him again, but he couldn't. Nonnie continued to live with Johnny, but Johnny continued to live alone.

CHAPTER THREE

Little upstairs room

Marcus sat in his little upstairs bedroom, his head resting on the misty glass, watching the torrential downpour outside. A thunderclap rattled the home, jarring Marcus out of his slumber and into consciousness. An exhilarating exhale accompanied his abrupt withdrawal from the window.

“Marcus?”

Taking his gaze away from the dismal landscape beyond his window, Marcus turned to look at his elder sister, Sophie, who stood at the entryway of the house.

"If you want to say goodbye to Mom and Dad before they go for work, that’s OK."

Following his sister down the stairs, Marcus nodded and risked a short glimpse back at his sister through the open window. A coat had been slung over his shoulders, and his mother was applying lipstick at the front door. As she looked in the mirror, she saw Sophie and Marcus coming down from the reflection. She grinned.

‘I haven’t seen you since the early hours of the morning. "Can you tell me what my little bee has been up to?" Marcus thought her voice sounded phoney. It caused his insides to twitch.

"I'm a fourteen-year-old mother. "You may no longer use that obnoxious moniker." Sophie mumbled under her breath.

Marcus stood there watching as his father walked around the corner. He was eating a cookie that had been stuffed halfway into his mouth, and he was also clutching an umbrella.

"Oh, Sophie! I'm so sorry! "Well, there you have it." His father attempted to say something, but instead ended up vomiting biscuit crumbs over the floor.

"Chris!" Marcus's mother burst out laughing. "I had just finished vacuuming the floor the day before."

"Please accept my apologies, Rachel." While stuffing the remaining biscuit into his pocket and grabbing his coat, he mumbled something else. Marcus's father swore as he looked at his wristwatch.

"I'm running late! For the third time this month, we've done it!" He kissed his wife goodbye after giving her a short embrace and brushing by Marcus in the hallway. Marcus's mother gave him a tight grin as the door slammed shut behind him. She took a big breath and glanced at Sophie and Marcus with a puzzled expression.

"I'm going to close the door behind me." Stay inside and don't let anybody in by opening the door, Sophie." Sighing, she reached for her vehicle keys and walked out into the rain, scowling at the gloomy weather.

With a loud clunk, the lock was slipped into position.

"Bye—" Marcus's words were welcomed with deafening stillness.

"I'm sitting in front of the television," Sophie stated.

Marcus stood there watching her take her laptop and make her way to the living room. He remained there for a long time, taking in the sound of rain pattering on the shingled roof and admiring the scenery. It was a nice respite from the tumultuous feelings that had been buried deep inside. Marcus walked the steps back up to the second floor, his socks making no sound on the carpet.

Marcus went inside his room and picked up his favourite Choose Your Own Adventure book, which he placed in the centre of the floor. He particularly like these sorts of novels since they had several endings to a single narrative. The room was suddenly lighted by lightning, which was quickly followed by thunder that rocked the home. Marcus read the book cover to cover, immersing himself in the protagonist's perspective.

Marcus was reading his book when the sound of rain ceased abruptly, and time seemed to have flown by. He walked over to the window, leaving his book on the floor behind him. The thunderstorm had gone on, but the cloud cover had stayed put for the time being.

"Marcus?"

Sophie stood at the doorway for the second time.

"Mom has returned."

Marcus merely gave her a nod, which was the only recognition he offered her. Sophie hesitated for a little while, opening her lips to say anything additional, but quickly decided against it and walked away. Marcus took a few steps away from the window, dropped his book on the floor, and headed downstairs to his room. His mother was in the kitchen, pouring herself a glass of wine, when he arrived. Close her eyes and droop her head as she leaned up against the counter and sighed.

Marcus left her there as he went in search of Sophie. She was lying on her bed, looking up at the glow-in-the-dark stars that had been permanently adhered to the ceiling. Marcus gingerly got onto the bed next to her and gazed up at the night sky as well as her.

"Have you ever wondered what it might be like to live up in the heavens?" says the author. Sophie muttered to herself.

“Yes.” He stated it plainly. "However, only if you are present with me." He turned his head to look her in the eyes, but she was already looking at him.

"I’d want to accompany you there as well." Sophie shared her thoughts.

They were peacefully lying there, looking up at the night sky.

Marcus eventually went off to sleep and awoke to the sounds of his sister and mother entering the house. Marcus saw that it was pitch black outside as he looked out the window.

"Good night, Mom," I say. Sophie remarked this while standing just outside her room. Marcus’s mother began to say goodbye as well, but she saw that the door to Marcus’s room was still open.

"Sophie, what’s with Marcus’s door being open? You’re well aware that I like to keep my mouth shut."

When she reached for the doorknob to shut the door, she saw the open book on the floor. She walked into the room and placed the book back on the bookcase, a sigh in her voice. Then she had a look around Marcus’s room and saw that the area could need a good dusting. She walked up to the window and glanced outside. The rain clouds had evaporated, leaving behind a night sky filled with glittering stars. The moonlight streamed down, illuminating the slick road in front of their home. Marcus’s mother shivered and swiftly averted her gaze away from the window in horror.

After walking across the room and slamming the door shut, she walked out of the room.

Marcus got out of Sophie's bed and went to the basement to get some fresh air. He didn't want to have to cope with Sophie's sympathy any longer. He exited the house via the front door and sat on the front porch stairs. He blinked frantically, trying desperately to keep the tears from streaming down his face. He clasped his hands over his ears, hoping for that refreshing shower to arrive, but it never came. The moon moved across the sky, and Marcus finally rose up to return to his room to rest. Even when he clutched the door handle and twisted, the door refused to move. Marcus slammed the door shut with his fist, enraged that his parents had locked him out again again.

He made his way around to the rear of the building and up the trellis to the roof. After passing his parents' room, he crept over the dripping shingles in the direction of Sophie's window. He took a breath and looked at them. It was evening, and his mother was reading against the headboard of her bed, while his father was in the bathroom, brushing his teeth. Nathan kept creeping and pounded on the window of Sophie's house. Before opening the door, her face showed in the glass, and she looked Marcus in the eyes for a brief moment. He snuck inside the house and landed on the luxurious carpeting.

"They've shut you out once again." Sophie made a statement.

Marcus kept his gaze away from her and nodded.

"Marcus." She let out a sigh.

"I'm not interested in talking about it." Marcus informed her that he was on his way out the door.

"No!" The tone of Sophie's voice halted him in his tracks in the middle of his stride.

"You can't keep deceiving yourself, Marcus," says the professor.

"I'm not," Marcus said, scowling at the ground.

"You certainly are!" Sophie expressed her displeasure. "You are Nathan Cross, my 10-year-old brother," says the narrator. You have a crazy obsession with the Choose Your Own Adventure series of novels. "You like kicking the ball around outdoors."

"You were killed in a vehicle accident six months ago, directly in front of our home. You are no longer alive. "You have to come to terms with it."

Marcus's shoulders trembled as tears streamed down his cheeks, which he'd been fighting so hard to keep back.

"Do you honestly believe I'm not aware of this?" Marcus spoke in hushed tones. "It's something that I'm reminded of every single day!"

Hugging him tight, warm arms wrapped him and drew him in closer. As Sophie began to weep, wet tears dropped across his head and into his hair.

"I'm a little worried, Sophie." Marcus leaned very close to her shoulder and sniffed.

"It's the same for me." She responded with a whisper and then a gasp.

"What?" Marcus inquired, taking a glance around.

"You're starting to fade, Marcus." Sophie gulped, her gaze fixed on the inside of Marcus's chest where her hands were. Marcus let out a cry and backed away from her grasp. Sophie tried her hardest to grin, but she failed spectacularly.

"I believe...

"I believe I'm ready to leave at this point." Marcus said this to her while looking into her eyes.

In a short period of time, his body was becoming more translucent.

"When you look up into the sky, remember me." Sophie informed him, her eyes sparkling with excitement.

“Bye—”

His words were welcomed with deafening stillness.

CHAPTER FOUR

Martha Cross

It was chilly, the leaves had just begun to change colour, and it was, in May Steven's view, the ideal time for a stroll. She'd spoken her goodbyes to her mother as she grabbed her coat on her way out, but her mother didn't appear to notice. However, there are no shocks there. Her mother was often preoccupied, whether it was one of her crocheted blankets or a new dish she'd been wanting to try; she had always seemed a touch distant, albeit not in a negative way. Mrs. Steven remained an incredible mother, always going above and above for important occasions, such as the holidays. She felt a little disoriented.

May proceeded on her way to her favourite hangout spot, the neighbourhood café. It was a serene setting, ideal for reading or studying. She has been several times to assist with school assignments. It was the only place she could escape her younger brother Josh's relentless nagging. Josh was the only one who could penetrate her defences in less than a minute. She still loved him, after all, he was her only brother, but he had an uncanny ability to get himself into all sorts of mischief. Whether it was peeking in her room or being caught slipping out to meet out with his mates, danger was always close by.

Her phone buzzed halfway to the café, and she dug it out of her pocket. It was a text message from her best friend Hailey. "Hey, I haven't heard from you in a while; are things all right?" While swiping to unlock her phone, she was unaware of the pedestrian approaching her. "Oof!" his shoulder brushed up against hers, almost knocking her down. The man glanced about furiously, almost as if he were staring straight through her. "Hey, be careful!" she whispered, "What the heck is going on?" He exclaimed, flailing his arms. He swiftly moved away, regaining his calm and continuing to ignore her presence. He was undoubtedly aware of colliding with her, yet he did not seem to see her or even hear her gasp when his shoulder collided with hers. That was ridiculous, wasn't it? She thought, truly, how could he have missed her? May shook her head in disbelief. The Cafe was just a few of blocks away at this point, and she could certainly need some coffee after the unusual meeting with the stranger. She was not easily frightened, and the fact that such a little matter had caused her such distress concerned her more than she liked to admit.

As she neared the cafe's entrance, the wind shifted, twisting the leaves and blowing the fragrance of roasting coffee beans her way. She was certain it would be a pleasant day. As she reached for the door, another person opened it, colliding with her and knocking her to the ground. The woman glanced around shocked, then back inside the store over her shoulder...and then walked away as if nothing had happened??? “Hey!! Keep an eye on your path; aren't you going to apologise?!!" May's auburn hair poured out of her hood and onto her face, causing her to choke whenever she spoke, as it usually did. She dusted herself up, restyled her hair into a ponytail, and entered the café, embarrassed. "Did you happen to see that, Mrs. Clearview!" It's as if they didn't give a damn!" She slammed the door shut and walked over to the counter. "Mrs.Clearview?? Hello??" Nothing, not even a grin or a wave in her way. May felt queasy; Mrs. Clearview was the cafe's proprietor, and May had always loved conversing with her whenever she visited to study. She had always been a fountain of knowledge and had never complained about assisting May with her schoolwork. "Hello?" she exclaimed, but received no response. She rushed towards the counter, arms flailing madly, terror engulfing her and suffocating her. "Mrs....... Mrs Clearview" Hello?!?! Hi!?!? Hellooo?!?!" Tears flowed down her cheeks, but no one in the store noticed or even glanced up.

Terrified, she took the only course of action that occurred to her. She snatched up her phone and attempted to contact her mother, but the phone became pale and fizzled in her grasp, "Oh my gosh, what is happening?!?!?!?!?" May sobbed as she turned around and dashed out of the store. This could only have been the result of a mental collapse. Perhaps she was having a mental breakdown after all? She'd spent the previous week cramming for her end of quarter examinations, which meant staying up until midnight on numerous evenings. She sped along the street, hardly pausing to take in her surroundings. She didn't pause for breath until she reached her driveway. "MOM!!!!! Something is wrong, Mom!!" She slammed the front door shut behind her as she entered the home. She paled, her mother sobbed in the kitchen, her father held her, and Josh stood transfixed in the corridor. "What is wrong, Mom!" Nobody responded when she yelled. Nobody raised their eyes, Josh didn't turn around; it was as if she didn't exist.

There was only one thing left for her to do; she rushed up to Josh and smacked him across the back of the head,

WHOOSH! Her hand pierced him completely. There was no deafening thud when her palm collided with his, and he didn't even turn his head to shout at her for striking him. She collapsed to her knees and sobbed. "Is no one hearing me?!?! MOM!!!! "IT'S ME, MOM!" she wailed. This was not conceivable, this could not be real; it had to be some sort of nightmare, one of those that seems genuine until you wake up sweaty from how near you came to death or how close the zombies in your dream came to devouring you. She began squeezing her arms. "Awaken, Awaken, Awaken!!!" She squealed. The environment remained unchanged; there was no startling awakening in her bed. Nothing.

May drew herself up and turned to face her family. She became aware that they were discussing something, no, not anything, but someone. They were discussing her. As she got closer, she could make out what her mother was saying between sobbing. "She's.. She is indeed gone, our precious baby child is truly gone!!! May is no longer alive!" Josh collided into the wall, his body trembling and tears streaming down his face. "NO!!! That is not correct!!! The nurse assured her that she would be OK, stating that it was only a concussion, nothing serious, and that she will awaken within the following day or two!!!" He yelled, his voice brimming with rage. May couldn't believe what was happening, and then it struck her: she had no recall of waking up, no remembrance of breakfast, and no recollection of getting out of bed. Dead? How was she able to die? She was standing just next them, but the more she thought about it, the worse she felt. This cannot be true! Could it be possible? Nobody appeared to be aware of her presence. This cannot be the end; she cannot be dead. There was no way... was this how death worked? Isn't she supposed to be floating? Isn't she supposed to be in a hospital room? Didn't her mother mention a hospital? May made a beeline towards her family. Her father was still holding her mother in his arms. "Honey...I...I'm not sure...get let's your belongings...we need to go to the hospital...we..." His words were drowned in the flood of tears. She had never seen her father weep in her whole 17 years. Not a single cry when their cat Lucy went away, not a single one when her brother destroyed his childhood baseball trophy.

However, now that he was unable to talk, she felt saddened. Her veins felt as if they were made of ice, and it took all she had to keep upright. "You're correct, Josh, put on your shoes; we're going to the hospital," her mother said. There was only one way for her to discover the truth, and that was to accompany them to the hospital. She followed Josh to the family minivan, slipping in behind him just as he shut the door. If this was a joke, the gag would have ended as soon as she went through the hospital doors; if it was a dream, it would have ended sooner; and if none of those were the case... May flatly refused to consider the third alternative.

Her parents boarded the vehicle moments later, and they were on their way to the hospital. "So...Did anybody realise I'm here? I'd really appreciate it if we could put a stop to this joke now," she paused, still getting no reaction from her family. She sighed as she realised she was about to go on the longest vehicle journey of her life. As they approached the hospital drive, her brother ripped open his door and dashed inside, providing enough chance for her to follow. As she passed through the doors, she saw a nurse accompanying him to the elevator. Her parents raced up after them, and the elevator was crowded to capacity. May gave the nurse a hopeful glance and a slight wave; she didn't appear to notice, so she reached out and gently prodded her on the arm. Nothing, her heart fell further. By the second, the odds of this being some crazy, twisted Halloween joke were fading. She was at a loss for what to do if she came into the hospital room and...wait a minute, the elevator was going down, not up, which could only mean one thing. They were on their way to the morgue, not the hospital.

Josh snapped his head around to face their father. "Dad, this is the incorrect route to the hospital rooms; this must be a mistake," he said to the nurse. "Ma'am, my sister is in a hospital room; you've made a mistake." " No, hun, I'm sorry; your sister died at 10:32 this morning and her body had to be taken to the morgue per hospital protocol," his face slumped. There was no denying it now; this was not a joke, and there would be no gleeful exclamations of "HA! We got you, we had you fooled good!" No, this was the genuine article; she was really deceased. It explained why no one noticed her, why the guy who had run into her was completely unaware of her presence, and why her phone had fizzled out of her fingers; after all, the dead had no need for technology. They had arrived at the lowest level, when the elevator bell sounded. She stepped out into the dimly lit corridor, sullenly trailing after her family in search of her corpse. After two left turns and a lengthy corridor, the nurse eventually brought them into a room with stainless steel doors, which was unmistakably the location of the dead.

"I understand this is a trying moment for you all, but please try to maintain your composure; this portion is difficult for everyone." She pulled through the door and saw Mays dead on a table. It was pale; her fingers had gone a faint steel blue, her lips had turned purple and were as icy as ice. There was no error. May moved in the direction of her body and felt a touch on her shoulder. She turned, and a figure of pure white light appeared behind her, swirling for a brief second before adopting the form of a red-haired female. "You may skip this section if you like; you are not obligated to remain; paradise is waiting." She extended her hand. "Are you sure this is it? I'm no longer alive? This is not how people claim it occurs" May crossed her arms and let her hand to fall to the side. "That is what everyone says, how did this happen, this is not what I expected" Her face darkened and she giggled. "Everyone believes they are going to paradise; NO ONE anticipates the darkness." Suddenly, her face got pale, her eyes darkened, big wounds emerged on her face, and her clothing became bloodied and faded. "NOW YOU ARE OURS!!!" She growled and sprang away from May, all pretence of friendship obliterated.

There was no time to think or react; she barely had time to look aside before being seized by the hand and jerked through the floor, the sounds of her family's frantic wails booming above her, and that was the end of Martha cross.

CHAPTER FIVE

Mr. Michael

As I strolled through the neighbourhood walkway, which was filled with brown leaves, the chilly wind blew on my cheeks, giving them a reddish red colour.

I walked with a light bounce in my feet as I made my way to my next-door neighbor's home, where he was an elderly guy in his seventies', Michael.

He was a guy who was grouchy due to the fact that he was confined to a wheelchair, yet he is a kind person. The first few times I went to his home, he tried to get me to leave, but as I persisted, it was clear that he was delighted that someone wanted to join him.

When I got close to his home, I decided to call it a day. I walked up to the front door and came to a complete halt just in front of it. With my hands, I brushed away the leaves and dust that had accumulated on my garments, putting myself in a presentable state before answering the door.

Prepared to be on the verge of falling asleep for an extended period of time, I anticipated an elderly gentleman slowly approaching the door while complaining before opening it.

To my surprise, the door was opened not long after I rang the bell. Was he waiting for me, as I suspected? When the door swung open, I said, "Michael, are you thrilled to see me?" I was kidding, of course.

It was a young guy who answered the door, not the person I had anticipated to see. He had brown hair and eyes, and he was dressed in a green cardigan with a blue shirt underneath.

He had facial traits that matched Michael's, but he was too young to be his son, so might he be his grandchild instead? It had to be since I recall Michael stating that he had a grandchild.

Hello," I said to the young guy who was still looking at me. "You must be Michael's grandson," I said. "May I inquire where Michael has gone?"

It was with a fast "It's for Michael," that I handed the present in my hand towards him, apologising that I hadn't prepared a gift for him as well. The individual didn't seem to have much of a response, and he seemed to be stupefied. He stayed deafeningly silence, as if he were not hearing me.

This is uncomfortable at the moment. "I thought to myself as I flicked my eyes towards him and then towards the inside of the home behind him, hoping to get a glimpse of Michael." "Thank you very much, Miss Maya. I really appreciate it. But..." After a lengthy period of silence, he finally spoke, but only halfway through his statement.

I muttered something in attempt to alleviate the uneasy mood "Is it possible that Michael has mentioned me to you before? And, if it's okay with you, I'll ask again: where has Michael gone?" I couldn't keep a grin off my face when I was saying this. That cranky guy really brought up my name in front of his family?

"Miss Maya, the 'Michael' you're talking about, is it 'Michael Beckwell,' my grandfather?" he said, his voice cautious and soft-spoken. "You don't even know what your own Grandpa's name is?" I said, furrowing my brows in displeasure.

"It's not like that, Miss." Then he got more reluctant, his voice sank, and his hands trembled as if he were recalling a memory he didn't want to recall: "My grandfather..." His voice trailed off after taking a deep breath. "He's been gone for 10 years, and you were at his burial, weren't you...?"

My face became ghostly white as the blood gushed out of it like a waterfall. Is Michael no longer alive? Since 10 years ago, what has changed? It couldn't be, since I just happened to see him......

I'm sorry, but my head aches. As I screamed and fell to the ground, I clutched my head hard in my palms of my hands. I could only vaguely recall the anxious tone in which she inquired as to my well-being. I was laying down on something gritty and listening to the sirens blare before I entirely lost consciousness.

I sat up in my hospital bed, stunned and speechless as the reality of what had happened suddenly dawned on me after many years of being buried deep inside my memory. My hands were covering my mouth and nose.

"How are you, Miss Maya?" I was awakened by someone calling my name, but I did not raise my hands to look at her and instead remained mute. "Miss Maya, I'm a licenced psychotherapist." I could hear someone shuffle their clothing and a chair being dragged.

"The hospital is able to draw the conclusion that your mental condition is unstable based on Mr Beckwell's claims. Is it possible that you should seek therapy?"

"Get out of here." I turned away from her and said, "I don't want to hear any of this foolishness right now." "Excuse me, Miss?" says the narrator. When my blood began to boil again, I flung my pillow at her and yelled, "Get out!"

I have no idea what occurred after that, and I have no desire to find out. I gazed out the window, taking in the beautiful sky and the chirping of birds as they passed by. "Do you enjoy this landscape, Michael?" "Do you like this scenery, Michael?"

In the perspective of others, I may seem to be speaking to nothingness, but to me, I am conversing with a person who is seated in a wheelchair beside me, a grouchy, elderly gentleman.

Printed by Libri Plureos GmbH in Hamburg,
Germany